Paisley Shirt

Paisley Shirt

Gail Aldwin

Chapeltown Books

British Library Cataloguing in Publication Data

A Record of this Publication is available from the British Library

ISBN 978-1-910542-29-3

This edition published 2018 by Chapeltown Books, Manchester, England

A number of the stories in this collection were previously published by the following: Alfie Dog Fiction, arial publishing, Bournemouth Poetry, Chapeltown Books, Ether Books, EVB Press, Flash-Fiction South West, Headlight Press, Ink Sweat and Tears, Paragraph Planet, Unbound Press/Spilling Ink, WWG Publishing

All Chapeltown books are published on paper derived from sustainable resources.

Contents

Paisley Shirt

It was a rapping on the front door that startled me from my newspaper. The knock-knock, tap, knock-knock was like Morse code. I fold the cover (ever since the *Daily Mail* went tabloid, I've never had a problem keeping the pages straight) then I go to check. Through the glass pane I see a spiked head of hair and a bright paisley shirt. Paisley indeed. Whoever wears paisley these days? Reminds me of the eiderdown I kept on the bed I inherited, that is, until I downsized to a single and packed the cover off to the charity shop. The knock-knock, tap, knock-knock comes again and tuning into the rhythm, I find my heart blundering. It can't be. I open the door. With his head cocked to the side, a star-shaped dimple springs onto his cheek. I am so taken aback I didn't know what to do. Before I have time to gather my wits, his arm is across my shoulder and I'm dragged into a hug. The button on his shirt digs into my chin and I get a whiff of cigarettes. 'You best come in,' I tell him. Standing straight against the wall, he brushes past me and along the corridor. He hasn't forgotten the layout of the house and heads straight for the kitchen. He slings his leather jacket over the back of the chair and crosses his legs so that the sole of one shoe rests on his knee. His body language is a bit too casual for my liking, and I stand there with my hands clasped. 'Sorry, Aunty Maggie,' he says to me and rearranges his legs so they fit under the table. 'That's better,' I say. It does no harm to remind these youngsters of their manners. There was a time when I had to entice him into the house with the promise of a biscuit. He came to like my shortbread and then it only seemed right to move him on to other wholesome food. After school, there'd be a couple of boiled eggs. I had to teach him how to slice off the top and scoop out the white. The dunking of soldiers was encouraged. If he finished every bit, then I'd offer him some homemade fool with redcurrants picked from the garden.

The teapot leaks a whisker of steam, and I arrange the cups and saucers. Lifting the milk jug, I wait for him to nod. There was a time when he'd only have black tea and I'd have to search the house over to find a bit of lemon to make the drink acceptable. His father was the same, snubbed his nose at the offer of milk. He didn't speak much English, not like the youngster who picked it up in no time. 'Are you called Piotr or Peter these days?' I ask him. He grips the handle of the cup, holding his little finger the way I taught him. 'Piotr,' he says. 'It was my father who liked to be called Peter.' I remember that well, back when I couldn't get my tongue around foreign words. 'He was a good man, was Peter.' It's nice to feel his name on my lips again.

We talk about what Piotr's doing, how he's made a success of his life. He went to university and got a first class honours degree. In English, would you believe? Then I remember the schoolboy who'd shrink from conversation. I was only being friendly when I first made an approach. Didn't like to think of him stuck at home. On his own, a bit like me. He'd have been called a latch-key kid in my day but what else could Peter do? He had to make a living, and on a building site the work starts early and finishes late. Peter made a point of going home to brush-up before collecting the boy. That was a measure of his respect. So on the occasion when he nodded his head towards my lounge, I didn't hesitate. I could hear chatter from the radio drifting as he cupped my neck in his hands. His kiss was warm. 'You want more?' he asked. And I did.

When Piotr is ready to leave he straightens the collar on his shirt then presses his arms into his jacket. 'You've turned into a snazzy dresser,' I tell him. He has that. Barely a trace of the boy remains. And the paisley pattern on his shirt is a bit like blind fish swirling. I guess the one with the puckered pink edge is me, lost in an ocean of nothingness ever since Peter's gone.

Breastfeeding

Hold the newborn in the crook of your arm and release your breast. Jab the nipple into the infant's mouth. If the child is not ready to feed, it may not open its mouth. In this case, press a finger on the baby's chin and wait for the lips to form an 'o'. Make sure the infant attaches properly. Where 'latch-on' occurs, the vacuum seals to ensure correct feeding. In cases where 'latch-on' fails, cracked nipples or seepage may result. Compensation for damage to breasts is only available to mothers who ensure that 'latch-on' is successful. A supporting letter from a midwife may be required as evidence in a claim.

Once the child has begun to feed, it is important that he or she receives the correct dose of milk. Do not let the infant fall asleep during feeding. It is natural for the child to appear drowsy but steps should be taken to ensure wakefulness. Try prodding the cheek or tickling the neck. When feeding has finished, remember to wipe the nipple with a damp cloth. The baby may require winding following breastfeeding. This can be achieved by holding the child in one hand and stroking its back with the other (a circular action is frequently effective). Alternatively, you may prefer to use a tapping or patting movement. When a burp is sounded, the process is complete.

Take care of your breasts and they will provide excellent feeding and service, birth after birth. There are no known side effects to breastfeeding, but if you experience your mood or mental health deteriorating, please contact a doctor immediately. Remember to continue feeding your child – formula preparations are not recommended.

Belemnite

The wind lashes my cheeks and strands of untamed hair escape from my scarf. False footed by the incline, I lose my nerve and shelter by the rocks. But Tommy strides the beach, his eyes fixed to the ground. Each time he shows a specimen to the expert, his shoulders hunch when the bearded man shakes his head. Other fossil hunters in flapping raincoats scurry like crabs, picking and turning pebbles. Screwed up with anticipation, Tommy continues to look, forcing over boulders too heavy to carry, examining the stones like jewels beneath. When it's time to walk back, he stiffens, shoving his hands in his pockets, shrugging off the arm I place around his shoulders. With his elbows sticking out like wings, he bends over and concentrates on searching with each step. The others wander off, but I stay and watch him, my face wet with drizzle. At a rock pool he drops to his knees, the water like obscured glass, he trails a finger through the weeds and shells. Removing a cylinder of black stone, he runs along the shingle to catch up with the guide.

As he walks back he smiles, his wet hair pointy and there's a glint in his navy rimmed eyes.

'It's a Belemnite, Mum.' Tommy places the bullet shaped fossil in my hand. I turn it over studying the surface marked with indents.

'Well done, Tommy. Now you can start a collection.'

'Naah.' He crinkles his nose. 'It's a present for you.'

At the Hostel

Jon hunched over the book and traced the double rose embossed on the cover. His nicotine stained finger showed a curve of dirt under the nail. Although the days of manicured hands were long gone, he did own a decent pair of nail clippers, somewhere. Finding the page with the corner turned, Jon squinted. He concentrated on the lines and practised reading aloud; the words were like jewels on his tongue. When he finished the verse, he tapped the cigarette packet until a filter appeared and he snatched the end. Rocking on the spindly chair legs, he took long drags and stared through the window looking for the edge of sky.

'I've got the shopping.' Bethany barged into the kitchen. Swinging the duffle bag from her shoulder, she slammed a tin of tuna onto the table. 'There's a loaf and some cheese. They were selling the last cuts of ham off cheap, so I bought a couple of slices.'

'We'll have a feast with that lot.'

'More like a couple of sandwiches. I'm starving. I missed breakfast and I'm dying for a cuppa.'

'I've got some teabags.' He pointed to the cupboard where he'd taken ownership by attaching a sticking plaster marked with his initials. It would be ripped off as soon as he left the hostel but in the meantime, it offered him the status of having a place to store his things. On tiptoes, Bethany fumbled a hand over the shelf. Thinking better of watching her struggle, he walked over and took down the packet then reached for the mugs. He counted the remaining teabags, enough to last his stay. He'd pass on all the things that he couldn't use on the street to Bethany. It wouldn't be much: half a bottle of shampoo and a few bits to eat. He'd keep the bar of soap and the disposable razors, he might get lucky in dodging the barrier at the swimming pool and be able to use the shower.

Bethany lined up the mugs and poured over the boiling water. Her T-shirt had shrunk and flapped halfway up her back. Jon studied the notches of her spine, then stole behind her, pressing his limbs to fit against her tiny frame. She rattled the cutlery drawer, searching for a spoon and Jon twisted his arm under her top. Through the slippery bra, he traced the circles of her nipples.

'You're not horny again.' She stirred the tea, slopping in milk and sugar. 'You got any money?'

'No. I gave you the last of my change for that food.' He sunk his chin onto her shoulder.

'Just checking.' She sucked the spoon, pulling it out of her mouth like a lollipop. 'You're going tomorrow, aren't you?'

'Yeah,' he sighed. 'I'll be leaving soon. An old schoolmate said I could kip on her sofa.'

'Will you miss me when I'm gone?'

'Of course,' she said. 'Who else will read me poetry?'

Greenhayes

'Christ, what was that?'

Frank doesn't answer but turns over, pulling the duvet with him. I roll out of bed and peek through the blinds.

'Sounded like a car backfiring,' I say.

'Not on Greenhayes. There aren't any old bangers around here,' says Frank.

I scan the cul-de-sac, looking for any sign of movement but it's quiet. The mock-Tudor houses stand in a row and our bay window offers a good view. I notice movement on the porch next door. It would be a foolish burglar trying to gain entry at the front. Reaching for my glasses, I see more clearly. There's a naked woman slumped on the doormat. Her tapered legs stretch to the step and her skin's silvery in the moonlight.

'Well I never.' I watch the woman hug her knees, trying to hide her breasts the size of honeydews. 'It's Jenny. Herman must've chucked her out.'

'I knew that marriage was never going to last,' says Frank.

'But it's the middle of the night and she's got nothing on.' I grab Frank's dressing gown and tie the belt around my waist, throwing the other robe over my shoulder.

'Blimey, what a woman.' Frank's at the window now he knows there's something worth watching. I stand beside him and we see Jenny shivering. 'You can't go interfering.'

'I'm only going to lend her my robe.'

'Herman went off his head when I cut a few inches off his precious leylandii. You don't want to make an enemy of him,' says Frank.

'I can't leave Jenny stuck on the porch like that. I'll never get a wink of sleep if I don't help her.'

I leave the house, my slippers clip-clopping as I walk to the boundary. The night is clear but the damp air clings. Standing on tiptoes I peer over the wall. She sees me and scurries through the shrubs. Passing over the robe I notice her fingers are like ice. She pulls a smile but looks set to burst into tears.

'Thank you.' Jenny's swollen top lip makes it hard for her to speak.

'Might stop you getting a cold – I'd invite you back but Frank says no. Won't hear of it after that last row he had with Herman.'

'It's okay.' She struggles to get her arms into the sleeves. 'Herman will let me in soon.'

'Okay then.'

I still can't sleep in spite of my good deed and when it's time to get up, I'm like a dishrag. Limping to the window, I draw the blinds and there's no sign of Jenny. She must've found refuge somewhere. When I get downstairs, there's a parcel on the back porch. I peel back the brown paper and there's my robe all fluffy and warm from the tumble dryer. There was no need to wash and return it so promptly. I find an envelope nestling by the collar and inside there's a thank you note from Jenny. She's signed her name in loopy handwriting and at the bottom, there's a smiley face. Only this smiley face has a black eye. I wonder if it's a coded message for help and I think about Jenny trapped in Herman's executive home like a modern day Cinderella but without a prince in sight. I look again at the smiley face and decide it's not a black eye just a blot from the ballpoint pen.

Hoping

Jet stumbles onto the treads then chases down the escalator. With his arms extended, he turns like a champion and beckons Liza to follow. She takes a step and glides towards him. As Liza tumbles against his chest, Jet swings his arm around her. They cling together and take each stride in time, heading towards the benches. She catches glimpses of their reflection in the shop windows, admires the way he's gelled his hair, wishes her legs were thinner in those short-shorts.

They sit together, their thighs touching, and Liza whips out a mirror to check her lipstick. While she's busy, Clara sidles up and Jet jiggles along the seat to make room, tapping the bench beside him. She takes her place like a foot servant to the king, and Jet shows Liza his back while he whispers in Clara's ear. Liza gets to her feet and wobbles on her heels then folds her arms and stares. Clara gets the message and slips away, pretending to look for a friend.

'I'll buy the cappuccinos.' Liza points to the cafe and squeezing her eyelids shut, she hopes to feel the weight of his arm across her shoulders.

Stone

The dining room is laid with paper cloths and napkins. In my pocket, the stone slips between my fingers, the surface smooth and cold. I found it in the garden as I shuffled along the path. I think of Laura and her clear gaze, her eyes watching my mouth as she tries to understand the words I dribble. I place the distorted heart on the table where she sits, a stone love letter.

Games

Tuesday morning

The vacuum cleaner rattles like bingo balls turning but when Sarah investigates she finds it's nothing more than a chocolate raisin caught between the blades. She sinks to the floor and sits cross-legged, shocked by the discovery. Holding her head between her hands, the tears drop, making a speckled pattern on the beige pile.

Last Saturday night

The springs on the couch twang under Keith's weight as he crushes the empty beer can in his fist. Five minutes ago he was nearly asleep.

'Get me another,' says Keith.

'That was the last one.'

'Christ. You could have stocked up. You haven't got much else to do.'

'If you say so,' Sarah sighs.

'Hey, I've got a another idea.' Keith lines up the chocolate raisins on the cushion so that they are positioned an inch apart. Making his thumb and first finger into an 'o', he practises a flicking action.

'Okay,' he says. 'Are you ready?'

'I'm tired.' Sarah stands but Keith grabs her hand and pulls her back.

'All you've got to do is chirrup for food like a baby bird.'

'I don't want to.'

'*I don't want to.*' Keith imitates. 'It's only a game.'

Sarah opens her mouth and waits for the pelting. Keith's not a very good shot and the chocolate raisins land everywhere but their goal.

'You're supposed to join in,' says Keith. 'Try to catch them.'

'I'm too tired for this. Let me go to bed.'

He dumps the bag of chocolate raisins on the side table and gropes beneath the wobbling mound of his belly. The zip rasps as he undoes his flies and Sarah realises what's going to happen. There are spikes in her blood, piercing.

'You'll open wide for this.'

The pounding batters her face and her heart beats so loudly the sound echoes in her ears. She'll die of suffocation and the thought terrifies. She can't leave Freddie alone with him.

Last Saturday afternoon

Freddie is in the bath, warming up after the outing. It doesn't matter that he fell in the brook, that's all forgotten. Sarah watches him as if through the lens of a camera: drops of water on his eyelashes, his curls flattened around his forehead. She reaches for a towel. It doesn't matter that Keith shouted. You have to when Freddie behaves badly. There aren't many husbands who help around the house, loading the washing machine with muddy clothes. He's a good man.

Last Friday

At the supermarket, Sarah studies the bags of sweets hanging from the rack. She chooses jelly sours for Freddie. The E-numbers will send him high, but who cares? It's the weekend. The offer says two bags for the price of one. Sarah selects another – this time she goes for something chocolate – Keith's favourite. It'll be a nice little treat while they snuggle on the couch, watching a film on TV.

Wreath

The apple tree bends, windblown with dotted clumps of green that thrive throughout the snow spilt days. My son was eight when he climbed the branches, pressed pearls from a Christmas wreath into the crevices of crinkled bark and waited. The parasite sprouted and each year, great globes of green appear against the leaf-stripped arms. Watching from the window, I admire the mistletoe's growth. By summertime, the infestation robs me of an apple crop. The tree fights water stress, maintains its place, a landmark on the hillside. If my son had been like the tree, he'd still be here today.

Accidental Brother

The television report shows bulldozers destroying shacks at the Jungle camp in Calais. I loosen my tie and unbutton the collar of my shirt. When the reporter asks a question, a young boy with a shock of dark hair speaks in my language. His words bubble and spawn. I aim the remote and switch the room to silence. As I walk to the kitchen, voices in my head scramble to be heard. I collect dirty plates from the counter and begin washing up. If only it was as easy to clear away the memories.

They scuttled through our village, beetles in armoured vests and tattered trousers. One wore a scavenged helmet. Their arms operated like pincers holding the guns. A species with no neck, heads balanced on shoulders. I can describe the scene minutely, every detail of their approach was captured in the seconds while I stood and stared. The game of Oware I played with Babik abandoned. The seeds I collected in my winning move, dropped from my fingers.

I was the kind of boy where instinct ruled. Had I thought, had I questioned, I would not be here today. Instead, a pulse in my ankle activated a response. I ran. Babik was at my side, his breath, my breath urging us forward. I didn't turn to look back. My bare feet thumped the ground, my heart beat like a hammer. Chasing me were the cries of women. I didn't see what happened to my mother.

When my throat burned and my limbs collapsed, it was beside Babik I fell. He was folded, covering his eyes. We didn't speak. That night we slept in some bushes and I tucked the sky around me as a cover. The next day, we walked. It wasn't clear where we were going, but we needed to walk, my accidental brother and me. We found water, we ate grass, we kept going.

There were others who joined us and we stayed in a line or bunched together. People talked about the soldiers: the way they killed and stole, took whatever they liked. I hoped my mother was crafty – that she was able to trick them and escape. I wanted her to be alive, to survive. The longing and need shredded my heart. Babik cried in his sleep, great gasps of fear.

'What dreams you have!' I shook him awake.

His eyes were wild. 'There were lions in the shadows, Kamal. The big one pounced. Its teeth ripped my legs, I could hear my bones crunching.'

'You're too skinny to be food for a lion,' I said. 'They have more sense than to eat a twig.'

Sometimes when we walked, Babik stayed silent so I talked with a doctor. He came from the south and he was still walking. Doctor talked about the future and asked what sort of job I'd do when I was grown up. I wasn't sure about anything, but I knew I wanted a family. That's when we heard a single scream of fear and pain. It frightened Babik and he ran into the crowd but me and Doctor went to investigate. We found a pregnant woman pinned to the ground, her belly bloated. She hid her face in a cloth and pleaded.

'Have respect for a woman in labour.' Doctor shooed the crowd away. He examined the woman. She whimpered. He stood and rubbed his forehead.

'I need a scalpel.'

The people shrugged and turned their backs.

'Can I help?' I asked.

Doctor nodded. 'Look in the dirt, by the track or near the trees. Search for something sharp.'

'Like a thorn?'

Doctor's face was marked with lines. 'The opening has to be bigger or she'll never deliver the baby.' He shook his head, seemed to be talking to himself. 'Girls who are cut, there are always complications. It's the price she pays for tradition.' Doctor cupped his chin in his hand. 'What are you waiting for? Get searching. Remember, anything sharp.'

I darted through the bushes, kicking up dust then I got onto my knees and poured grains of dirt through my fingers. When I found a shard of glass, I raced over to Doctor. 'Will this do?'

We left the woman nursing her child. Her clothes were stained with blood. We had to keep walking. Safety was within our grasp, two hundred miles, perhaps.

'Will she be okay?' I asked.

'If she lives it will be thanks to God,' said Doctor. 'If she dies, she will not be alone.'

I lost my accidental brother that week or the following one. He sank to the ground and hugged his knees. I didn't know how to make him keep going. I pushed him, tried slapping him, but he wouldn't move.

'Look at the girls. They're still walking,' I said.

Babik turned his head and stared into the distance.

'I'll sing a song if you walk with me.'

Flies collected around Babik's cracked lips.

'I'll find you food.'

Babik closed his eyes.

'Please don't give up, Babik.'

He keeled onto his side. He was the shell of the boy from my village. 'Goodbye, my friend, my accidental brother.'

I had to walk away. I wanted my life but Babik had stopped wanting his.

When I came to a village, the people gave me dried meat. I thought it was bark from a tree. I'd never tasted anything like it. The salt made my lips smack. I chewed until it was soft and it slithered into my stomach. The food and the water made me strong. I was ready to walk again. There were rumours about a camp where I could find shelter. Some said there was a school and a hospital. I followed the prints on the ground made by the men and women who had taken the route before me, the small footprints of children, too. I had hope. It powered my legs, helped me ignore the pain. After months of walking, I found a safe place and eventually, I made it to Europe.

I stack the dishes on the draining board but there's one plate with a stubborn mark that I can't remove. It's there to remind me of Babik. My accidental brother will accompany me always.

Graft

When your life disintegrates, you become a fragment of the person you used to be. The purpose you used to have. You remember waking in the morning, sunlight filtering, Margaret's breath thrumming a tune. You savour the ritual of selecting a tie and the challenge of a double knot. Tea served at the dining table in a china pot. The newspaper delivery and the snap of the letter box as you collect it.

Your place at work is elevated and the staff who knew you from school are no longer friends. What did you care? You run a schedule, acquire a secretary and oversee the budget. At the end of the month, the boss'll invite you for lunch, where you'll swallow oysters with a smile, but your stomach revolts. Your success brings whiter teeth, coifed hair and a tan from that regular holiday. These are luxuries that make the stress of the job worthwhile.

So what can you do when your life is decommissioned? You drink the tea that Margaret offers and when the post arrives, you add another rejection to the pile. You're glad of the dining table, a new place to toil, and you complete a fresh job application.

Burnt Toast

The smell of burnt toast reminds me of my grandmother. I can see her leaning out through the open kitchen window and scraping the crusts so that the dark flakes fly. The charred slices are placed in a gilded rack and she carries the makings of breakfast through to the dining room on a lacquered tray. My grandfather sits swathed like a surgeon in white linen, the tablecloth drapes to his ankles and a napkin is tucked into the collar of his shirt. Grandma pours tea through a strainer to catch the leaves and she adds a measure of milk from the jug. A silver spoon tinkles as it slides around the saucer. Eating commences when the toast is slavered with butter and dolloped with marmalade. The bread is a cold and brittle remnant from its torching, and the slices are hard to cut. Half of my breakfast dashes off the plate when Grandma attempts to make the toast into a child-sized piece. Dismissed from the table, and with my readied slice in hand, I hunt for the itinerant end. Creeping under the table, I lean against the pedestal and make a start on the toast. I have to suck the blackened edge until it crumbles then I'm ready to chew. The butter is salty against the bitter strips of marmalade. It doesn't take long to devour the lot. If I was sat with my grandparents I'd get a telling off for playing with my food, but under the table there's no one to see. When the breakfast things have been cleared away, Grandma is on her hands and knees, hoicking the end of cloth and peering into my secret place.

'Did you find the lost bit of toast?' she asks.

'No.' I shake my head and my plaits whip my shoulders.

'Never mind, wait till elevenses. There'll be more food then.'

Grandpa has a choice of special outfits that are fit for gardening. Today he wears a light blue jumper with a hole at the elbow and there's a ladder running up his middle like he's been cut in half. He loads the wheelbarrow and trundles it to the flower beds beyond the lawn. His dahlias have blooms the size of dinner plates and when the flaky petals fall, it looks like fairies have shed their wings. I check the forest of stems and call to the fairies in a singsong voice but they never leave their hiding place. When a frog jumps onto the path, I stand very still and watch him winking.

'Yoo-hoo, yoo-hoo.' A voice travels from over the garden fence.

'Morning, Winnie.' Grandpa digs his spade into the earth and leans on the handle. 'Come to say hello to my special helper, have you?'

'I thought I heard the youngster.' Winnie's bright pink lips match the baubles on her necklace. 'What are you doing, Susan?'

'Finding frogs,' I say.

'Chase them this way. They've got no business leaving my pond.' She launches her hand through the shrubs and between her fingers something silver glints. 'Have a Club biscuit – don't tell your grandma.'

It's time to water the plants on the terrace and angling the spout, I douse the roots. They need a good drenching because the weather's been dry but the watering can is heavy, so Grandpa finishes the job. I follow the path round to the side of the house where the kitchen window is swung open. I step onto a slab that's black and shiny.

'You're standing on a unique exhibit.' Grandpa smiles. 'It's taken decades of scraping toast to create Grandma's work of art.'

Wedding

The guests gathered on the terrace to see the newlyweds off, and Sally fussed about her dress. She'd ripped the trim when she trod on the hem and the bodice was ill-fitting since she lost all the weight. Of course it was Anna who caught the bouquet, and she lifted it like an Olympic torch, then flashed a fuchsia smile in Sally's direction. Ignoring her, Sally waved as the car crunched along the gravel drive all the way to the gatehouse. Rod unbuttoned his collar and tucked the silk cravat into his pocket.

'I fixed the car with a kipper under the bonnet, put it right by the air vents,' he said.

'Very inventive.' Sally blew the stray strands of her fringe away from her face. 'Your speech was… entertaining.'

'Yeah.' Rod necked the remaining champagne from a glass abandoned on a table. 'I'll bring the car round to the front and then I'll say goodbye to Anna. Can you be ready in ten minutes?'

'Fine.' She watched him swagger in the morning suit, imagined the conceited smirk on his face.

Sally collected the overnight bag from her room and Rod slung it in the boot. She fiddled with the buttons on the CD player, then turned it off. The silence between them pricked.

'When shall we tell them?' asked Sally. 'We can't keep delaying. We'll need to say something before they start showing the wedding photographs.'

'After they're back from honeymoon. That's the right time.'

'It's been a dreadful day. The way they kept going on about following the example of their best man and bridesmaid.' Sally frowned. 'Will you collect your stuff by the end of the week?'

'If that's okay,' said Rod.

'Yes, and I'll instruct a solicitor.'

Baby Blues

Lining up the bottles of baby formula, I thank God for the respite of when she's asleep. An adult's company is a bonus, even if he's only come to fix the boiler. Alex raps his knuckles on the worktop. The back of his hand is smattered with freckles and his skin has the syrupy shade of a light tan.

'I'll be back to do the service next year. Thanks for the coffee.' He counts the notes that I offer and folds them.

'You mean I've got twelve months to wait until I see you again?' Tilting my head I notice his red hair is streaked with grey, rather more silver than gold. He smiles, making his eyes soft. I bite my lip, resisting the urge to smile back and Alex lingers, the silence holding us. Moving closer, he angles his head to reach my lips. His bristles scrape as he works his tongue and I wrap my arms around his neck. When saliva seeps onto my chin, I nudge his elbow and step away. Studying the lines of laminate on the floor, I straighten my shirt.

'I can drop by one day next week.' Alex arranges the tools in his belt.

'That isn't such a good idea, there's the baby to think about.'

'And your husband, or is he a boyfriend?'

'She's my partner, actually.'

'You mean I just kissed a dyke?'

He tosses the spanner in his hand and aims it at the window. Stepping back as the glass shatters, his blood speckles the paintwork. My shoulders cinch and I'm frozen in place. Slamming the door as he leaves, air seeps through the broken glass. I force my limbs to work, tiptoeing to avoid the shards and I stare through the jagged hole. Alex is on the pavement. He swings his head from side to side, as if he's checking for witnesses and a few moments later, the van drives away. I'm left wondering how to explain the damage but the baby's still asleep, so I have time to plan.

At the Restaurant

Ushering us to a table in the corner, the waitress passes the menus while I lower my great bulk onto the chair. Dan sniggers as I stroke my belly, and I place the napkin on top like a doll's handkerchief.

I order a rare fillet steak owing to my condition and Dan chooses a bottle of red on the same pretext, a fine wine from St Emilion. I take my time devouring the food then wait for the signal. When Dan raises his eyebrows, I push my chair back. It scrapes the tiled floor, signalling for the chatter in the restaurant to become hushed. Dan necks the last of the wine and I head for the loo.

Patting my face with a wad of damp toilet paper, I rehearse the line. With my dress hanging limply over the globe of my stomach, I struggle back to the table.

'My water's broken.' I speak in a voice loud enough for everyone to hear. Dan jumps to his feet and flaps his arms like a chicken in fright then he clutches my elbow and we limp across the restaurant. The waitress is only too keen to wave us out through the door with no mention of the bill.

Dan laughs as he puts the car into gear and I rip the padding from under my dress.

'Another free dinner,' says Dan. 'Only next time, let's wait until I've had my pudding.'

Triathlon

'Gary's done everything you've asked. He's upstairs now, studying. You should believe in him not check his every move,' says Mum.

'You can't trust a boy whose been hooked by a brunette,' says Dad.

'No wonder he's taken to cycling and swimming. He needs to escape from under your glare.'

'There's nothing wrong with showing an interest.'

'You made sure his relationship with Fabienne ended weeks ago,' says Mum. 'She's back with her family now, where she belongs.'

Mum's words tarnish her name. Gary closes the window, doesn't want to hear any more. Instead, he remembers Fabienne's lips, her strawberry breath. He curls his fingers, imaging her hair in his grasp, the weight of her head against his shoulder. Moving to the bookshelf, Gary takes the atlas Granny gave for his birthday. The middle pages show the British Isles and Gary focuses on the wash of blue that colours the sea to France.

It's later that spring when Dad drops Gary at the athletics club and loads his bike onto the trailer. He hands the driver a fiver to pay for the ride, then slaps Gary's shoulder and heads home. Talk on the minibus buoys Gary's confidence: there's a chance of winning the youth category of the regional triathlon, but Gary has other hopes.

Where the cycle path runs alongside the coast, Gary abandons the bike. Against his heart is taped a photo of Fabienne. He traces the square edge through his top then plunges into the sea.

In the Highlands

Droplets fall in parallel lines and the rain plinks against the earth. Banana leaves fan the mist, and beneath the covered balcony of the lodge, there's activity in the kitchen. I'm startled by shouts in Tok Pisin then I concentrate, trying to make sense of the words. Elias appears barefoot in the doorway and watches the downpour; his springy hair shows a scattering of flour. He lights a cigarette rolled in newsprint and takes a long drag. 'Im bagarap.'

'Bugger up, indeed.' I assume he's referring to the weather, but it could be a disaster in the kitchen, judging from the smell of burning that wafts. He disappears inside before I have a chance to practise my conversational skills, not that he really wants to talk to me. It's easier being with the women in Papua New Guinea. They chatter and stroke my hair with fingers thin as vanilla pods.

When the sun splits the clouds, I walk to the edge of the gully. The land is covered in a lemon light and the river is a piece of twisted foil. In a clearing, little children emerge from kunai houses, squat wooden buildings with smoke seeping through the thatch. One boy is naked but for a belt of twine strung around his middle and his head's been shaved. The hair is used to make ceremonial wigs which the tribesmen decorate with bird of paradise feathers. I have at least learnt something during my study tour.

'An-i-ta.' The three syllables of my name bounce over the distance from the lodge. I return to find Elias with his hands cupped. Whatever he's holding,

I hope it isn't alive. Last night a moth the size of a sun hat had me cowering under the covers.

'Lukim yu.' He hands me a clump of moss and the roots of an orchid show. The flower hangs delicate between the leaves. I lean close to breathe the scent of honey.

Elias's smile is broad and his brown eyes dance. 'Nais.'

'Very nice.' The flower nods as I examine the structure and the dotted markings on the waxy petals. I find words of thanks in Tok Pisin, 'Tenkyu.'

Elias shows me how to strap the orchid to a tree and each day I walk the garden to admire the plant. The gift is an entry into his world.

Assignment

Leanne throws a cushion at Katy then snatches the remote. That'll teach her. Flicking through the channels, Leanne decides there's nothing suitable for her little sister to watch.

'Read your book,' says Leanne.

'Make me.'

'It's that or helping with dinner.'

Katy folds her arms and scrunches her face like she's all disgusted.

'Here.' Leanne tosses her the remote and smiles. It's important to keep on friendly terms. She needs to act normal even though her heart thumps.

She wanders into the kitchen where her mother stands at the stove. The whole place reeks of fried food and Leanne turns up her nose.

'Stop that,' her mother taps Leanne's wrist, 'if the wind changes direction.'

'I'll be stuck with this expression.' Leanne selects a knife from the drawer. 'What can I do?'

'Scrape the carrots, please.' Her mother swallows onion tears. 'How was your day at school?'

'I got an 'A' for my assignment.' Leanne tops and tails.

'You're a good student, Leanne. That's what your form tutor says.'

'School's about working hard.' Leanne's lips creep into a smile, the lies come easily these days. 'I've got revision tonight. Big test soon.'

'In that case, you leave the cooking to me.' Her mother holds out her hand and Leanne places the knife in her palm. 'Put your studies first, my girl.'

In her bedroom, Leanne wedges the chair against the door. She heaves the blankets from under the bed and grips the holdall hidden behind. Undoing the zip, Leanne checks the contents. Pressed and folded are her clothes, the outfits chosen to complement Sim's style. She finds the negligee with the lacy trim, lets the fabric slip through her fingers. Owning something like that is proof she's more woman than schoolgirl. Her mind fills with bubbles of excitement that blot out fear. When you're proper in love, there's only one path.

The challenge of the morning will be to stay calm. Sim says she has a pure soul to match his sincere heart. Nothing can go wrong. She has the savings she's cleared from her bank account and with her passport safely in her bag, there'll be no one to stop them.

When Leanne has packed everything away, she sits at her desk and traces the messages written in her exercise book. They are code for a secret future. There's no point in studying the GCSE guides that line her shelf. Leanne rocks on the chair and stares through the window at winking stars. She'll look at the same sky in Spain, but her life will be totally different. At school, everyone calls him Sim, the mister abandoned in classroom banter. She'll have to get used to addressing him differently.

'Andrew.' His name tastes sweet. 'I can't wait to be with you.'

Turning Tables

James sipped the glass of wine to steady his nerves. He'd hardly touched the food even though he'd helped to choose the menu. Emma had managed a couple of bites of salmon then she'd spun the silver cutlery around the rim and pushed the plate away. Grappling with the linen tablecloth and the napkin that wouldn't stay put, James reached for her hand. She slid her fingers between his and he toyed with the ring, newly in place.

Over on the round table, his mates were necking the free wine. A bottle of white was upended in the ice bucket and several bottles of red were empty. Des's tie hung limply around his collar, his jacket was slung over the chair. His appearance was similar to the days when they walked to school together, although he tended to wear long trousers these days.

At school, James had sat on the square table, along with Timmy who wore National Health specs, and Jenny whose nickname was two-chairs owing to her size. With his pencil tucked behind his ear, James was always ready to write. But when the exercise books were passed around, he found the lead was blunt and his ideas had vanished. Mrs Marshall said his handwriting was like a spider's scrawl and he rarely earned a house-point. In the weekly spelling test, Des managed to get full marks and the diamond table shot up the score board.

Emma leaned over and whispered in James's ear. Glancing at his watch, he knew the time was right. He stood and surveyed the room: the tables were spread before him and when Emma clattered a spoon against her glass, the guests turned to face him. Des waved his arm, gesturing for the boys to quieten down, and he gave James a wink. Smiling back, James needed no encouragement. It was his turn for a place at the top table and he savoured the moment.

Aethopian Maid

With fingers like cinnamon quills in shape and colour, Clara runs them over the embroidered hem of the green silk gown where clusters of pansies in gold and silver thread nestle. Clara checks the fabric, a task she undertakes each spring when moths are wont to cause damage. A scent of herbs and lavender pervades. Dried flower heads fall from the folds as she checks the seams and gathers. Her mistress prizes this gown more than the others and work is needed to keep it fresh. Clara carries the gown on its pole and hangs it outside in the breeze of the warm spring day.

Taking a dry rod, Clara beats the silk, turning the gown until it is clean and perfectly dry for storage. She takes it to the bedchamber of her mistress and prepares to hang it alongside the other, lesser gowns. Before she does, Clara holds the dress against her. The sage silk is bright against her blackamoor skin. The hem falls around her ankles for she is taller than her mistress and less stout. She dances with the gown pressed to her and thinks of the boy who smiles at her often. He is a lad who works in the stables, but he has a strong, straight spine and he's honest, they say. Clara thinks he will be bold. She may never wear a dress of fine silk, but she will marry him, one day.

Lipstick

On the windowsill of Mum's bedroom there's a lipstick, a globe-shaped bottle that smells of apricots and a necklace with a shiny heart. Mum sleeps on a mattress but I have my own room with a proper bed and a pink rug. Her room is like a racing track and I skip around the walls ready to leap across the finish line. When I land in the hallway, Mum startles and water slops from the bucket. She's on all fours and looks like Speedo, Granny's cat. It's a pity we don't live near Granny any more. I go to Mum and stroke her hair, but she hisses when my fingers catch the tangles.

'I'll make hot chocolate when I've finished cleaning – you have to wait, Lexi.' Her lips are turned into a smile but her forehead is creased. 'Try not to make so much noise.'

Out of Mum's window, the buildings look the same as the ones in London but living here we don't have to share our kitchen and bathroom any more. I want to throw my ball and watch it bounce to the ceiling, but I have to be quiet. Taking Mum's lipstick, I twirl the end until a red candle shows. I press it against my lips to smear the wax, but it snaps. I show the stub of lipstick when Mum comes for me.

'That's my only one.' Her eyes are like headlights. She grabs my wrist, bundles me along the passageway and out the front. Cold from the pavement goes right through my socks. I can hear crying but she doesn't answer when I knock. My head is full of worries that spurt like foam. If I set off now, I'm sure I can walk all the way to Granny's. She'll know what to do.

Barbecue

From the terrace, the Sydney Opera House is a white spider against a duvet of silky black night. I'm living in a world of negatives. Girls turn their backs when I approach, the ties on their bikini tops dangle along their spines.

'You best join the line, mate. Wait any longer and they'll run out of tucker.' The hostel worker nods towards the barbecue where smoke wafts as meat on the grill spits. I grip the cloakroom ticket. It says 373. I turn my mind to calculating and the numbers soothe.

I exchange my ticket for a plate. The guy uses tongs to sling a steak onto the cool ceramic. I need a roll to make a burger but I haven't got any bread. Standing still, I think about what to do next.

'Move along, mate.' The Aussie with thick eyebrows wipes sweat from his face with the back of his hand.

'I want to make a burger.'

'There's bread in the basket.' He points to a table by the wall. 'Come on, I'll show you.'

The Aussie hands me a container of ketchup and I squirt just the right amount of sauce. When I bite into the burger, my teeth marks make perfect semicircles.

'Where you from, mate?' he asks.

'London W5.'

'Right-oh. Is that anywhere near Shepherd's Bush?'

'No,' I say. 'But I change Tubes there on my way to college.'

'Cool.' He slaps my shoulder in a friendly way. 'I lived in Shepherd's Bush for a year. Seems we've got something in common.'

He stands beside me as I finish eating.

'You like kangaroo?' he says.

'The big red at Taronga Zoo is 1.8 metres tall.'

'I mean the steak.'

I shake my head.

'It was kangaroo steak.'

I throw the plate like a Frisbee. There's nothing else I can do when I live in a world of negatives.

Plant a Foot

His paper face is threaded with fine red lines, a result of drinking wine served in large glasses. Discretion makes him order a small one, this time. My husband jostles through the crowds to reach the bar. The man coughs into curled fingers then wipes his hand on the back of his jeans. I look at the floor. *Don't mind me,* he says. I twist my lips into a smile, trying to be friendly with someone I'd rather not know. *Your other half's not a bad cricketer.* I lean against the wall, my spine's ready to collapse. A full day of sitting on the boundary has me exhausted. *Best score of the match, he got.* The man drains his glass and places it on the shelf beside me. I shuffle sideways for a breath of air and he stares. *So what are you doing, these days?* He taps his foot, waiting for an answer. *I work with refugee children.* Beads of sweat slide from his temples. *Didn't you used to be a teacher? What are you doing wasting your time with them?* The vein on his neck pulses. *I am a teacher. The kids need to learn English, get some qualifications, help them to find a job.* He shakes his head then flattens the fallen strands of hair back into place. *You've got to be kidding me.* The tirade begins: *We're overrun with them, can't cope with more people. We live on a tiny island.* I fix my eyes to stare at him, all puffy and sweating. Blotting out the words, I watch his lips move. He sneers and sniffs. If for one moment, he could plant a foot in their shoes, he might feel differently. *God love you, mate.* He reaches for the glass my husband passes.

Packing

1. Clothes
   a. Tops: shirts and hoodies
   b. Jeans: ripped, skinny, bootleg
   c. Skirts: mini, maxi, puff
   d. Bras: underwired and padded
   e. Knickers: pretty ones only
   f. Shoes: heels, flats, Converse
2. Make-up (ditch dried-up nail varnish)
3. Jewellery (silver-dip before packing)
4. Hairdryer and straighteners
5. Pencil case
   a. Highlighters
   b. Gel pens
   c. Retractable pencils
6. Ammonite found at Charmouth (wrap in tissue – put in box with flowers on lid)
7. Paperback (any)
8. Pillowcase with broderie anglaise trim
9. *Foxy Lady* mug
10. Remember: thermal socks, hot water bottle, Blue Ted, ring binder with campus information

Friends

Most of the boxes are unpacked and when I've finished cleaning my bedroom, I'll put up the last of the curtains. The hems will hover above the sills but they'll remind me of our old house, of our old life. I screw the newspaper into a ball and swipe it over the just-washed window, removing the streaks and smears. When my arm begins to ache, I balance on the ledge and stare outside. My son's walking home: his shirt's tucked in but for a flap at the side. The tie is his only form of self-expression and he wears it showing a tiny knot and a long tail. With his mates, he barges along the path, bags swinging. He shouts goodbye as he turns towards our front door and I hear the key in the lock.

Peeling off the rubber gloves, I call downstairs and follow my voice as it bounces off the walls. Entering the kitchen, I see Ben taking gulps from the milk bottle.

'Use a glass,' I say.

'There's no need, I'm going to finish it.' He lands the empty bottle on the table.

'Good day at school?'

'Yeah, I suppose.'

'You looked happy walking home. Who were those boys?'

'Ollie and Sam – they live round the corner.'

'Oh.' I think of the times I've nodded and smiled at the neighbours but they don't make newcomers feel welcome around here. 'You've got your dad's knack for being friendly. He'd have been proud of you.'

'I know.' Ben smiles and moves towards me, his arms outstretched. 'Have a hug. You'll soon get to meet people.'

'I'm not so sure.' While I'm smothered in his arms, a tear seeps. I wipe it away as he releases me and I hide my face. 'Have you got any tips for making friends?'

'Nobody's ever asked me that before.'

I stare at the wall and talk to the cobwebs. 'I need to know because I'm desperate.'

'Don't worry, Mum, it'll be okay. Just try talking to someone, anyone.'

'I'm not sure I can do that.'

'Or you could try walking into them – make it look like an accident – and start a conversation from there.'

'Good idea.' I disguise a giggle by starting to cough. 'I better get on with sorting my room.'

'You can do it,' Ben calls after me. 'I know you can.'

Through the sparkly glass, I watch the walkers on the street. A grey-haired woman swings a plastic bag with dog poo inside while the puppy pulls the lead and sniffs the grass verge. There's a man dragging a shopping trolley behind him. Holding her toddler's hand, a mother finds a gap in the traffic to cross the road. I imagine using Ben's accidentally bumping into someone strategy, and laugh. The curtains need hanging and I get on with the chores.

Blue Skies

Sitting here in my plaid skirt, you'd never guess I had an adventure when I was young, back when me and Ned were newlyweds. He's been gone twenty-five years and I've spent more of my life as a widow than a married woman. Shame of it was he had such a zest for life. Came home one day, bursting with plans for his promotion to the head of department at a new comprehensive. Wasn't long before he had to take sick leave and they pensioned him off early owing to the cancer.

I first noticed him at the train station wearing a swanky sweater and two-tone brogues. He wanted to take me to Brighton for the day. I had to stare out of the window most of the way because I couldn't return his gaze. Said he was transfixed by me. Can't think why. I was nothing more than a typist fresh out of the commercial class and he was older and a teacher at the grammar. Next plan was to get wed double-quick, not that I was pregnant or anything but he wanted to take a chance on going to Australia.

The sky in the southern hemisphere is something you never forget. The blue is liquid-bright. Provides optimism for the day, for the life you've got. I was never happier than to get away from the heavy-on-your-eyebrows London grey. And there was something tuneful about Australia. Sitting on the veranda at night, listening to the rhythm of cicadas or hearing the wind ripple through the gum trees that built to a crescendo when the storms came.

I worked in the kitchen at the boarding school where the dishwasher churned and the ovens belted but I never complained about the heat. While I stood at the sink, I watched the kids launching into the swimming pool, cooling off after a morning of lessons, larking about. Later, it would be me and Ned taking a swim. We'd wait until stars pricked the sky and go skinny-dipping, our bodies sleek, his wet skin sliding against mine. Okay, so he took the key without permission but no harm was done until the girl with sun-bleached hair made an issue. She stood in the principal's office and pointed at Ned, accused him of doing stuff. Not that I was there, but I could imagine the scene from the way Ned told it. The girl's parents moved her to another school but that didn't stop the mutterings and it was rumoured that Ned would never get another job in the Australian school system, not with a mark like that on his record. The principal promised a good reference if we headed back to the UK. Least that way we could claim to be ten-pound tourists, not loving Australia as much as we thought, wanting to get back home.

My secretarial skills came in handy when I had nothing more to live on than a widow's pension. Had to get all togged up for work in a suit and I resented wearing stockings after the days of bare legs and cotton shorts in Queensland. My life has changed since I retired and I became a volunteer at the local primary school. Funny how things turn out, isn't it? I go there every afternoon and listen to the little kids read. It's amazing how quickly they pick it up with some extra help. Mums and dads don't have time for sharing stories these days but I love it. I never go into the juniors, mind. I'm not interested in the older children and don't want to be reminded of girls who lie. You can never trust the blonde ones. At times like this when you can't see the sky for slate tiles, I really hate her.

Little Brother

Gary sits in the armchair with the Sunday paper. The reading lamp pours light onto the print so he can read without squinting. Over on the couch Jenny's resting – it's been another disturbed night but that's not surprising with a new-born. The baby's called Joshua but he's already known as Josh. At least the name bears resemblance to the original. Who would guess Nim's birth name was Imogen? Not that it matters. Six years old and she's a proper little person: self-contained, responsible. She knows to hold Josh's head when she cuddles him and she's the only one who can sing him to sleep. This makes Jenny feel inadequate but she can't complain as she's swimming through fog.

Turning onto her back, Jenny stares at the water mark on the ceiling. The bathroom leak happened months ago but Gary hasn't bothered to paint it over. It's good that Nim's contented. Give her a picture book and that'll occupy her for hours. She points to the words but makes up the sentence. During the last couple of days all the stories have included a brother. They must've done something right, Jenny and Gary, to have a daughter who loves the baby so much.

'Want a cup of tea, Jenny?' Gary lumbers to his feet.

'A glass of water will do. Can you get Nim something to eat, as well?'

Nim sits cross-legged on the carpet, waiting. She's hasn't got much patience so she goes over to check on Josh. When she tucks the yellow blanket around his body, Josh opens his eyes. He's not pretty like a doll but he waves his arm like he's saying hello.

'You're my little brother,' says Nim. 'And I promise to look after you always.'

Also By Chapeltown Books

Spectrum
by Christopher Bowles

A collection of one hundred and ten pieces of flash-fiction and poetry. You probably won't like all of them, and some of them might even disgust you, or make you uncomfortable. But stick with it. Look at overarching themes within each coloured block. Find the puns in certain titles. Research the colours that you've never heard of. Try and work out which stories are complete fabrications, which ones contain nuggets of truth, and which ones are versions of real life events.

Order from Amazon:

ISBN: 978-1-910542-13-2 (paperback)
978-1-910542-14-9 (ebook)

Chapeltown Books

Fog Lane
by Neil Campbell

Fog Lane is a collection of stories about memory. Many of the stories have been published online and in magazines. They were written over a long period of time. The oldest, *The Rose Garden* was first written in about 2007 and published in Orbis. The last one in the book, *Here Comes the Sun*, was completed in 2017. The stories in this book vary from the humorous to the sad to the macabre. They are all short stories of under a thousand words.

Order from Amazon:
ISBN: 978-1-910542-08-8 (paperback)
978-1-910542-09-5 (ebook)

Chapeltown Books

Potpourri
by Anusha VR

Potpourri is an eccentric mix of stories and poems. Somewhere between working twelve hour shifts at a tax firm and cramming for exams, these stories and poems tumbled onto torn sheets and paper napkins. Potpourri is an attempt at preventing the literary world slipping away and regaining a sliver of that bookish world.

Order from Amazon:

ISBN. 978-1-910542-21-7 (paperback)
978-1-910542-22-4 (ebook)

Chapeltown Books

Badlands
by Alyson Faye

A collection of flash fiction pieces, from drabbles of 100 words to longer pieces up to 1000 words. They reflect an interest in ghost stories, history especially the Victorians, old movies, derelict buildings, real life issues such as homelessness, and just the 'what if' factor of when a seemingly normal situation starts to tilt off centre, dangerously so.

A surprising collection of creepy tales. Tales so twisted, you won't want to read them at night. I didn't, I read them in an afternoon. They are brilliant
(Amazon)

Order from Amazon:

ISBN: 978-1-910542-25-5 (paperback)
978-1-910542-26-2 (ebook)

Chapeltown Books

www.ingramcontent.com/pod-product-compliance
Lightning Source LLC
Chambersburg PA
CBHW080753120626
46557CB00005B/1258